I Love My Hair

by Anne Matheson

Illustrated by
Amanda Savo

Every life is special.
Every life is full of things to love.
Some people might think Emily's life is ordinary.
They might think her hair is ordinary...
or too curly...or frizzy.
Not Emily...

I love my hair!

Every morning, Emily gets up early, looks in the mirror, and sings:

It's **BIG,**
and it's *curly.*
And no one
else has hair
like me!

And I LOVE MY EYES!

They're **BIG**, and they're **round**, and they see the whole world. And no one else has eyes like me!

And I LOVE MY MOM!

She's nice, and she's funny.
Last night she tucked me in and said,

"GUESS HOW MUCH I LOVE YOU?"

And no one else has a mom like me!

And I LOVE MY DAD!

He's **STRONG**, and he's nice. He plays soccer with me and my friends. He makes me pancakes. And no one else has a dad like me!

I LOVE MY HOUSE!

I LOVE MY ROOM!

I LOVE MY DOG!

I LOVE MY BROTHER!

And no one else is just like me!

but I do when it's a sunny day and we read books outside.
And no one else has a teacher like me!

And I LOVE MY FRIENDS!

We like to skip,

we tell stories,